MY ALLAH SERIES
ALLAH LIVES FOREVER

Kisa Kids Publications

If a candle's wax melts, it no longer gives light.
The flame disappears, and it becomes dark at night!

What will happen if there is no light?

4

Everything in this world needs something to stay alive,
Let's look around and figure out why!
If a flower isn't watered, its petals become dry.
They slowly start to fall, and the flower begins to die.

What do all plants need to live?

PARENTS' CORNER

وَتَوَكَّلْ عَلَى الْحَيِّ الَّذِي لَا يَمُوتُ

And rely upon the All-Living, who will never die
(Sūrat al-Furqān, Verse 58)

Dear Parents/Guardians,

As children grow older, they ask many questions to try to understand Allāh. On one hand, it is important to introduce to children Allāh's attributes, such as His Wisdom, Power, and Knowledge. However, on the other hand, it is important for children to understand that Allāh is not like us. He is not comparable to anyone or anything.

One good way to highlight that Allāh is unlike human beings is to realize He is the One who has given us our lives. This will create the foundation for children to realize that He is the only One worthy of worship because everything we have is from Him and we are solely dependent on Him and only He is independent. He is the only One we can rely on and ask for help. Therefore the very first step towards realizing His greatness is to understand that He is incomparable to other beings.

With Du'as,
Kisa Kids Publications

In order to live, chickens need food like grains.
If they don't eat, they start to feel pain!

What are some healthy foods Allah made for us to eat?

A bird gets hurt if it flies into a tree.
It can break its wing and even start to bleed!

But did you know that Allah will never die?

6

Allah is al-Hayy — He will always be alive!
He does not need anything to survive.
Allah doesn't need water to live like the flower.
He created water, and with it, gave life and power.

Where does rain come from?

Allah isn't like the candle that needs wax to give light.
He made the wax for the candle, so it can shine bright!

What other creations of Allah give us light?

8

Allah isn't like animals that need food to stay alive.
He created this earth with food so they can survive!

What are some foods Allah created for animals?

Allah can't get hurt or feel pain like a bird. He doesn't have a body, so He can't get hurt!

Who can help us when we get hurt?

Allah created us all, every boy and girl.
He brought us to life, and to Him we'll return!

What are some creatures Allah has created?

11

Say it with me: Laa ilaaha illallaah.
Which means there is no god except Allah!
He gave us everything we have, every blessing in our life.
Every gift is from Allah, who will always be alive!

What are some blessings Allah has given us?